A Note to Parents and Caregivers:

With a focus on math, science, and social studies, *Read-it!* Readers support both the learning of content information and the extension of more complex reading skills. They encourage the development of problem-solving skills that help children expand their thinking.

 The PURPLE LEVEL presents basic topics and objects using high frequency words and simple language patterns.

 The RED LEVEL presents familiar topics using common words and repeating sentence patterns.

 The BLUE LEVEL presents new ideas using a larger vocabulary and varied sentence structure.

 The YELLOW LEVEL presents more challenging ideas, a broad vocabulary, and wide variety in sentence structure.

 The GREEN LEVEL presents more complex ideas, an extended vocabulary range, and expanded language structures.

 The ORANGE LEVEL presents a wide range of ideas and concepts using challenging vocabulary and complex language structures.

When sharing a content focused book with your child, read to find out facts and concepts, pausing often to restate and talk about the new information. The realistic story format provides an opportunity to talk about the language used, and to learn about reading to problem-solve for information. Encourage children to measure, make maps, and consider other situations that allow them to apply what they are learning.

There is no right or wrong way to share books with children. Find time to read and share new learning with your child, and pass on the legacy of literacy.

Adria F. Klein, Ph.D.
Professor Emeritus
California State University
San Bernardino, California

Editor: Shelly Lyons
Designer: Abbey Fitzgerald
Page Production: Michelle Biedscheid
Art Director: Nathan Gassman
Associate Managing Editor: Christianne Jones
The illustrations in this book were created with acrylics.

Picture Window Books
151 Good Counsel Drive
P.O. Box 669
Mankato, MN 56002-0669
877-845-8392
www.picturewindowbooks.com

Printed in the United States of America.

All books published by Picture Window Books
are manufactured with paper containing at least
10 percent post-consumer waste.

Library of Congress Cataloging-in-Publication Data
Emerson, Carl.
The busy spring / by Carl Emerson ; illustrated by Cori Doerrfeld.
p. cm. — (Read-it! readers: Science)
ISBN 978-1-4048-2625-0 (library binding)
ISBN 978-1-4048-4756-9 (paperback)
1. Spring—Juvenile literature. I. Doerrfeld, Cori, ill. II. Title.
QB637.5.E44 2008
508.2—dc22   2008007172

The Busy Spring

by Carl Emerson
illustrated by Cori Doerrfeld

Special thanks to our advisers for their expertise:

Dr. Jon Ahlquist, Ph.D.
Department of Meteorology, Florida State University
Tallahassee, Florida

Adria F. Klein, Ph.D.
Professor Emeritus, California State University
San Bernardino, California

PiCTURE WiNDOW BOOKS
Minneapolis, Minnesota

Emma woke up and looked outside.

The streets were wet with melting snow.

Emma got dressed. She wanted to get to the park quickly.

Owen was standing next to Old Oak.
He was waiting for Emma.

"Hello, my friends," said Old Oak.

"Hello, Old Oak," said Emma and Owen.

In North America, the season of spring begins in March. It ends in late June. The seasons of summer, autumn, and winter follow.

"Spring is here," said Old Oak.

The air warms in the spring. Each day, the sun climbs higher in the sky.

"All living things are busy now."

Emma and Owen climbed Old Oak.

There were lots of tiny bumps on
Old Oak's branches.

"What are those bumps?" asked Owen.

"The bumps are called buds," said Old Oak.

Trees make buds in the spring. The buds will turn into leaves.

Rachel the robin landed on one of
Old Oak's branches.

"I am finishing a nest for my babies," Rachel said.

Most animals have babies in the spring and summer.

Emma and Owen wanted to see the baby robins. They saw only eggs. They would have to wait.

The next day, Emma and Owen went to the park. Still, they saw only eggs in the nest.

Two weeks later, Emma and Owen
went to the park again. They ran to
Old Oak.

23

Emma and Owen looked at the nest.
They did not see the eggs.

"The babies are here!" Emma and
Owen yelled.

"Yes, they are," said Old Oak.

Emma and Owen watched the hungry babies chirp.

"The babies need to eat," said Rachel.

"Soon it will be summer. Then the babies will be on their own," said Old Oak.

Fun Spring Activities

You can do lots of fun things in the spring. Here are some ideas:

- Visit a nature center or park. While you are there, go on a nature hike or scavenger hunt. Watch all of the new life that arrives in the spring.

- Adopt a park with your family, friends, or classmates. Clean it up to celebrate Earth Day on April 22.

- Make a bird feeder. Fill it with birdseed for all of the returning birds.

- Plant a tree to celebrate Arbor Day on the last Friday in April.

- Visit a local farm or zoo and see all of the new spring babies.

- Go to your local library. Check out some books and CDs about birds and their calls. Try to learn about at least three birds.

Glossary

bud—a flower or leaf that hasn't opened yet
melting—changing from a solid to a liquid; like ice changing to water
robin—a bird with brown feathers on its back and orange feathers on its face and breast
season—one of the four parts of the year; winter, spring, summer, and autumn
spring—the season after winter and before summer

To Learn More

More Books to Read

Carr, Jan. *Splish, Splash, Spring.* New York: Holiday House, 2001.

Glaser, Linda. *It's Spring!* Brookfield, Conn.: Millbrook Press, 2002.

Jackson, Ellen B. *The Spring Equinox: Celebrating the Greening of the Earth.* Brookfield, Conn.: Millbrook Press, 2002.

Lenski, Lois. *Spring Is Here.* New York: Random House, 2005.

Roca, Núria. *Spring.* New York: Barron's Educational Series, 2004.

On the Web

FactHound offers a safe, fun way to find Web sites related to topics in this book. All of the sites on FactHound have been researched by our staff.

1. Visit *www.facthound.com*
2. Type in this special code: 1404826254
3. Click on the FETCH IT button.

Your trusty FactHound will fetch the best sites for you!

Look for all of the books in the *Read-it!* Readers: Science series:

Friends and Flowers (life science: bulbs)
The Grass Patch Project (life science: grass)
The Sunflower Farmer (life science: sunflowers)
Surprising Beans (life science: beans)

The Moving Carnival (physical science: motion)
A Secret Matter (physical science: matter)
A Stormy Surprise (physical science: electricity)
Up, Up in the Air (physical science: air)

The Autumn Leaf (Earth science: seasons)
The Busy Spring (Earth science: seasons)
The Cold Winter Day (Earth science: seasons)
The Summer Playground (Earth science: seasons)